DINO PAJAMA PARTY

DINO PAJAMA PARTY

- A BEDTIME BOOK -

Written by **LAURIE WALLMARK**

Illustrated by **MICHAEL ROBERTSON**

RP|KIDS
PHILADELPHIA

Running Press Kids
Hachette Book Group
1290 Avenue of the Americas, New York, NY 10104
www.runningpress.com/rpkids
@RP_Kids

Printed in China

First Edition: October 2021

Published by Running Press Kids, an imprint of Perseus Books, LLC, a subsidiary of
Hachette Book Group, Inc. The Running Press Kids name and logo is a trademark of
the Hachette Book Group.

The Hachette Speakers Bureau provides a wide range of authors for speaking events.
To find out more, go to www.hachettespeakersbureau.com or call (866) 376-6591.

The publisher is not responsible for websites (or their content)
that are not owned by the publisher.

Print book cover and interior design by Marissa Raybuck

Library of Congress Control Number: 9780762497751

ISBNs: 978-0-7624-9775-1 (hardcover),
978-0-76249776-8 (ebook),
978-0-7624-7110-2 (ebook),
978-0-7624-7109-6 (ebook)

APS

10 9 8 7 6 5 4 3 2 1

FOR TOBY—L.W.

TO MY LOVELY MOM, CARMELINDA.
LOVE YOU FOREVER.—M.R.

Dinos rock, and dinos roll.
Dinos stomp, and dinos stroll.

All the dinos on the street boogie to that funky beat.

Dinos roar,
and dinos shriek.

Dinos boom,
and dinos squeak.

Dinos singing extra loud
rush to join the dino crowd.

Dinos plink,
and dinos strum.

Dinos toot,
and dinos drum.

Dinos come from all around
just to play that rocking sound.

Dinos swing,

and dinos shake.

Dinos leap, and dinos quake.

Dancing dinos sure have fun
Jiving 'neath the setting sun.

Dinos yawn,
and dinos drag.

Dinos droop,
and dinos sag.

Dino toes are getting sore.
All the dinos leave the floor.

No more rocking out today.
Sleepy dinos trudge away.

Snug in bed,
they dance no more.

Fast asleep,
the dinos snore.